LOOKING AT
COUNTRIES

Looking at
CHINA

Jillian Powell

Gareth Stevens
Publishing

Please visit our web site at: www.garethstevens.com
For a free color catalog describing our list of high-quality books,
call 1-800-542-2595 (USA) or 1-800-387-3178 (Canada).

Library of Congress Cataloging-in-Publication Data

Powell, Jillian.
      Looking at China / Jillian Powell. — North American ed.
            p. cm. — (Looking at countries)
      Includes index.
      ISBN: 978-0-8368-8169-1 (lib. bdg.)
      ISBN: 978-0-8368-8176-9 (softcover)
   1. China—Juvenile literature.   I. Title.
   DS706.P69   2008
   951—dc22   2007003004

This North American edition first published in 2008 by
Gareth Stevens Publishing
A Weekly Reader® Company
1 Reader's Digest Road
Pleasantville, NY 10570-7000 USA

This U.S. edition copyright © 2008 by Gareth Stevens, Inc.
Original edition copyright © 2006 by Franklin Watts.
First published in Great Britain in 2006 by Franklin Watts,
338 Euston Road, London NW1 3BH, United Kingdom.

Series editor: Sarah Peutrill
Art director: Jonathan Hair
Design: Storeybooks Ltd.

Gareth Stevens managing editor: Valerie J. Weber
Gareth Stevens art direction: Tammy West
Gareth Stevens graphic designers: Charlie Dahl and Dave Kowalski

Photo credits: (t=top, b=bottom, l=left, r=right, c=center)
Paul Barton/Corbis: 21. Claro Cortes IV/Reuters/Corbis: 23. Bernd Ducke/Superbild/A1 Pix: 17, 26.
Ric Ergenbright/Corbis: 15b. Haslin/Sygma/Corbis: 24. Jon Hicks/Corbis: 11b, 18t, 20t. Earl and Nazima
Kowall/Corbis: 12. Bob Krist/Corbis: 9t. Photocuisine/Corbis: 20b. Carl and Ann Purcell/Corbis: 15t.
Keren Su/Corbis: 1, 7t. Keren Su/Lonely Planet Images: 10. Superbild/A1 Pix: 6, 7b, 9b, 11t, 18b, 22, 25t, 27b.
Superbild/Haga/A1 Pix: 13, 19, 25b. Superbild/Incolor/A1 Pix: front cover, 4, 8, 16, 27t. Peter Turnley/Corbis: 14

Every effort has been made to trace the copyright holders for the photos used in this book. The publisher apologizes,
in advance, for any unintentional omissions and would be pleased to insert the appropriate acknowledgements in any
subsequent edition of this publication.

Printed in the United States of America

1 2 3 4 5 6 7 8 9 11 10 09 08 07

Contents

Words that appear in the glossary are printed in **boldface** type the first time they occur in the text.

Where Is China?

China is in eastern Asia. It is the fourth largest country in the world after Russia, Canada, and the United States.

The capital city, Beijing is in northeastern China. Beijing is one of the largest cities in China, with more than fifteen million people. The city is more than three thousand years old. It has lovely **temples**, palaces, and parks alongside modern skyscrapers.

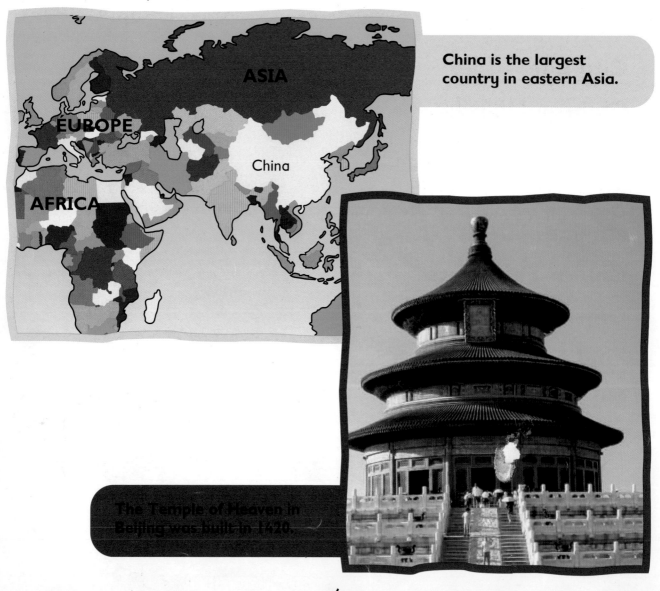

China is the largest country in eastern Asia.

The Temple of Heaven in Beijing was built in 1420.

This map shows all the places that are mentioned in this book.

China borders fourteen countries including Russia, Mongolia, and India. Its coastline runs along the Pacific Ocean, the Yellow Sea, the East China Sea, and the South China Sea.

Did you know?

The Chinese often call their country *Zhongguo*, which means "the Middle Kingdom."

The Landscape

China has many different kinds of landscapes, including sandy deserts, rocky plains, **subtropical** forests, **swamps**, and high, snowy mountains. The highest mountains are in northern and western China. They surround the Tibetan Plateau, a huge area of high land where little grows.

The Great Wall of China stretches over 3,700 miles (6,000 kilometers) over mountains, deserts, and river valleys. The wall was built to keep China's enemies out. It took hundreds of years to finish.

A girl works in terraced rice paddy fields in Longji.

Less than one-fourth of China's land can be farmed. The most **fertile** farmland is in central and eastern China. There, rivers bring water to the wide plains. **Terraced** fields are cut into the hillsides for growing crops, including rice, tea, and vegetables.

The Yangtze is the longest river in China.

Weather and Seasons

Much of China has a mild climate, but there are big differences between the north and south. The weather in northern China is colder and drier than in the south. Little rain falls, and icy winds blow in from Siberia in winter. In the northern Gobi Desert, it can be very hot in the summer. Temperatures rise to 113 °Fahrenheit (45 °Celsius). They can drop in the winter to -40 °F (-40 °C).

Camels carry goods across the Gobi Desert.

Did you know?

In parts of northern China, snow falls for 150 days each year.

People cool off in a fountain in Hong Kong in the south.

Most of southern China has a **tropical** climate, with warm weather and lots of rain all year round. In the Himalayan Mountain ranges of southwestern China, however, the climate is **subarctic**. The summers are short, and the winters are long and cold.

In the summer **monsoon** season between May and September, strong winds and heavy rains blow in from the Pacific Ocean. **Typhoons** can hit the southeastern coast between July and September, causing damage and flooding.

A couple wears the traditional outfits of Tibet, where the climate is subarctic.

Chinese People

More than 1.3 billion people live in China. Most are Han Chinese. The Han people have lived there for more than four thousand years. They speak a language called Mandarin Chinese.

There are also more than seventy million people from other **ethnic groups** in China. These groups include Mongolians, Tibetans, Zhuang, Jinuo, and Miao. Each group has its own language, **culture**, religion, and traditional clothing.

A crowd gathers for a festival in the Guizhou region.

Did you know?

One out of five people in the world are Chinese.

Religious traditions and ceremonies are important in everyday life in China. Some people practice folk religions. They worship different gods and goddeses. Other people are **Buddhists**, **Taoists**, Muslims, or Christians.

The Jinuo live in the mountains of Yunnan. Jinuo women are known for their beautiful weaving.

A group practices tai chi in a park in Shanghai. Tai chi is a popular system of exercise across China.

Family and School

Most Chinese people greatly respect older people and their **ancestors**. Grandparents often live with or near their grandchildren. They often help working parents by looking after the children. In turn, families often care for their older relatives at home.

At the festival of Ching Ming, families remember their ancestors and picnic next to their graves.

These children in Xinjiang Uygur in northern China will learn to read and write one other language besides Chinese.

Most children start school when they are six years old. They usually attend school for nine years. The school day usually begins at 8 a.m. and ends at 4 p.m. Many schools have ten minutes of physical exercise before classes begin.

Did you know?

June 1 is Children's Day in China. Children go to many fun activities instead of attending school.

Country Life

More than two-thirds of the people in China live in villages and work in the countryside. Some people have small plots of land where they grow food for their families. They also sell some food at markets. They may keep a few animals, such as pigs, chickens, or ducks.

This couple, who live in the Sichuan region, are carrying pails of water for their crops.

Farmers prepare flooded fields for planting rice. They are using oxen, which are a kind of cattle.

Most farmers plant and harvest crops using hand tools and animals to help them. Some farmers now have tractors for plowing fields and carrying food to markets to sell.

In northern China, most farms grow crops such as wheat, millet, or soybeans. South of the Yangtze River, where the climate is warmer and wetter, farmers grow tea and rice.

Farmworkers pick tea leaves near Hangzhou.

City Life

Just under one-third of the people in China live in cities. Many Chinese cities are very crowded, with several million people living in each. The largest cities are Shanghai and Beijing, the capital. They are busy, modern cities with many skyscrapers. These huge buildings contain offices, homes, stores, and restaurants.

People crowd this busy shopping street in Shanghai.

Many people bicycle to work in Chinese cities.

People have lived in the Beijing area for over two thousand years. Today, the city contains long shopping streets, outdoor street markets, and old areas of narrow alleys called *hutongs*. Factories, malls, and huge modern buildings have been built around the city center.

Did you know?

Tiananmen Square in Beijing is the largest public square in the world.

Chinese Houses

In the crowded cities of China, most people live in small apartments in groups of skyscrapers. Some schools, factories, and companies provide homes for their workers in these apartments. In the older areas of many cities, houses were built around **courtyards**. Today, many of these houses have been divided into smaller homes.

Hong Kong workers live in these blocks of apartments.

These traditional houses in Beijing are built around a courtyard with a small garden.

These old country houses in southern China are built from the local stone.

In the country, most houses have one story and are built from mud, clay bricks, or stone. In places that often have heavy rains, homes are built on raised platforms to help keep them dry.

Did you know?

Some people in China live in cave homes. Others live on houseboats called *sampans*.

Chinese Food

Many kinds of fresh food are sold in markets like this one in Beijing.

Rice forms the basis of many dishes, especially in southern China. In the north, wheat is made into bread, noodles, and dumplings called *jiaozi*.

Many regions have their own special dishes and styles of cooking. In Sichuan and Hunan, the food is hot and spicy. In southern China, dishes include sweet-and-sour pork and dim sum, which are steamed or fried dumplings made of flour and water.

Dim sum are often served in little baskets and eaten as snacks.

Chinese children learn how to use chopsticks from their parents and grandparents.

Both steaming and stir-frying are popular ways of cooking food in many parts of China. Meals are eaten with **chopsticks** and are often served in several small dishes. Sharing meals together is an important part of family life.

Did you know?

Chinese children eat noodles on their birthdays to bring them luck and a long life.

At Work

About half of the Chinese people work in farming. In the country, many people cannot find work, so many people are poor. Many younger people are moving to the cities to find jobs in factories or offices.

This woman is decorating a vase in a **porcelain** factory.

This factory makes plastics and chemicals.

Chinese factories make machinery, cars, aircraft, clothes, electronic equipment, plastics, and **ceramics**. They also produce iron, steel, and gas. The number of jobs is increasing in movie theaters, hotels, restaurants, and stores in China's busy cities.

Did you know?

The Chinese invented paper and fireworks.

Having Fun

Chinese people like to keep fit. Badminton, volleyball, table tennis, and kite flying are all popular sports in China. Most schools and factories support sports teams made up of students or workers. People also enjoy board games, such as Chinese chess, and **mah-jongg**, which is played with tiles.

Did you know?

Some Chinese kites are so large that they need several people to fly them.

These badminton fans are supporting China's team at the Olympic Games.

The Beijing Opera performs all over the world. Opera stars dress in colorful costumes and makeup.

Chinese opera, acrobats, and circus performers are famous all around the world. Many Chinese acrobats started training as young children.

Chinese festivals include feasts, music, parades, and fireworks. The most important festival is Chinese New Year, which is in January or February.

Dancers dress as lions or dragons for parades during Chinese New Year.

China: The Facts

• China is a **Communist** country called the People's Republic of China. The president is head of the government, and power is held by the leading members of the Communist Party.

• China is divided into twenty-three provinces, five regions, and four major cities. Each area elects members of the National People's Congress, which makes the laws in China.

• With more than 1.3 billion people, China has the largest population of any country in the world.

China's flag has yellow stars on a red background.

Gleaming skyscrapers fill Shanghai's international banking and trade district.

The Chinese currency is the renminbi, which means "the people's currency."

Did you know?

More people in the world speak Mandarin Chinese than any other language.

Glossary

ancestors – family members who lived long ago

Buddhists – people who follow the teachings of Buddha, who lived from about 563 to 483 B.C. The religion of Buddhism is followed throughout central and eastern Asia.

ceramics – objects made from fired clay or porcelain

chopsticks – long sticks used for eating

Communist – describes a system of government that tries to create a country where everyone is equal. The government owns all businesses and land instead of individuals.

courtyards – spaces next to or in the middle of homes, palaces, or other buildings

culture – the way of living, beliefs, and arts of a nation or a specific group of people

ethnic group – a people who share a common origin, culture, or language

fertile – having rich soil that is good for growing crops

hutongs – narrow alleys

mah-jongg – a popular Chinese game played with sets of tiles

monsoon – winds that come at a specific time of year carrying heavy rains

porcelain – smooth, white pottery

subarctic – the kind of landscape or climate found next to the Arctic Circle where it is very cold

subtropical – relating to land near the Tropics and describing areas that are wet and warm

swamps – flat, wet lands

Taoists – people who follow the beliefs of Taoism, which are based on the teachings of Lao-tzu, who lived in the sixth century B.C. in China

temples – buildings used for prayers and religious services

terraced – describes land that is cut into steplike levels or fields

traditional – descibes ways and beliefs that have been passed down through a group over many years

tropical – describing warm, wet regions of Earth that are near the equator

typhoons – violent tropical storms

Find Out More

Ancient China
www.historyforkids.org/learn/china

A to Z Kids Stuff: China
www.atozkidsstuff.com/chinal.html

Time for Kids: China
www.timeforkids.com/TFK/hh/goplaces/main/0,20344,536982,00.html

Holidays and Festivals: China
www.studyzone.org/testprep/ss5/b/comholchinal.cfm

Publisher's note to educators and parents: Our editors have carefully reviewed these Web sites to ensure that they are suitable for children. Many Web sites change frequently, however, and we cannot guarantee that a site's future contents will continue to meet our high standards of quality and educational value. Be advised that children should be closely supervised whenever they access the Internet.

My Map of China

Photocopy or trace the map on page 31. Then write in the names of the countries, bodies of water, regions, cities, and land areas and mountains listed below. (Look at the map on page 5 if you need help.)

After you have written in the names of all the places, find some crayons and color the map!

Countries
China
India
Mongolia
Nepal
Russia

Bodies of Water
East China Sea
Pacific Ocean
South China Sea
Yangtze River
Yellow Sea

Regions
Guizhou
Hunan
Sichuan

Xinjang Uygur
Yunnan

Cities
Beijing
Hangzhou
Hong Kong
Longji
Shanghai

Land Areas and Mountains
Gobi Desert
Himalayas
Mount Everest
Tibetan Plateau

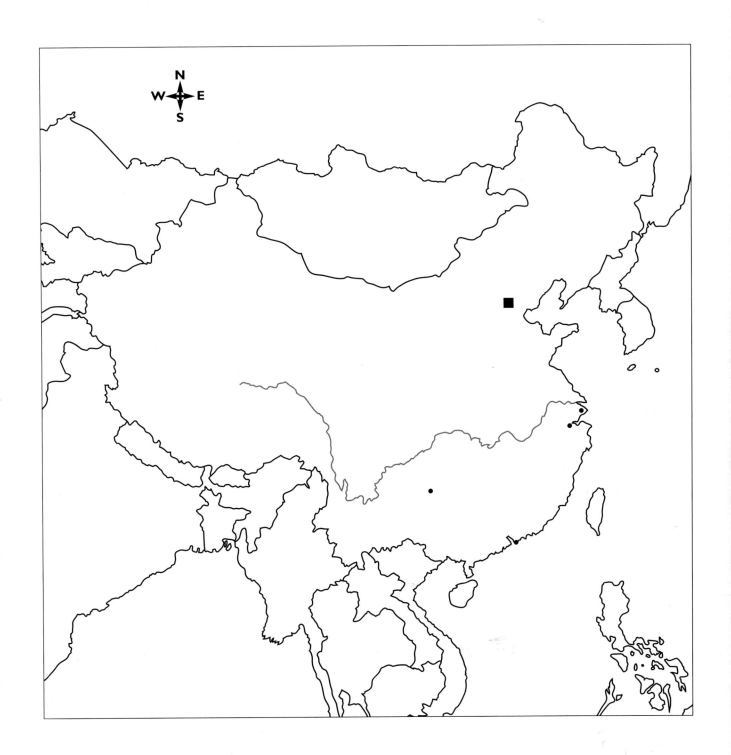

Index